Dot
and
Bob

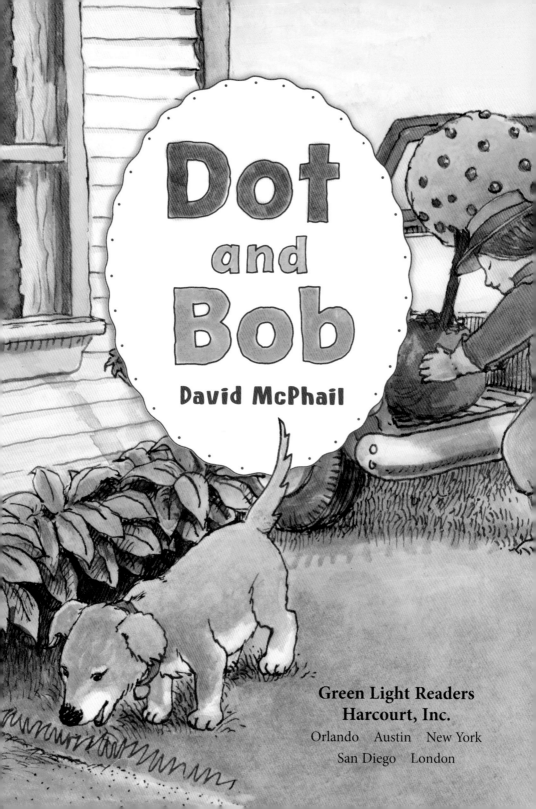

Dot
and
Bob

David McPhail

Green Light Readers
Harcourt, Inc.

Orlando   Austin   New York
San Diego   London

Bob is Dot's dog.

Bob likes to dig.

Oh, Bob! Do not dig there!

Mom has a tree.

Dot will help Mom dig.

It is hot.

It is too hot to dig.

It's not too hot for Bob!

Bob likes to dig.

Bob digs down, down, down.

Did Bob dig too much?

Mom will find out.

Look at the treetop!

Bob kicks and kicks.

Now the tree fits.

Thank you, Bob!

What Do You Think?

Who is the character
that helps Mom and Dot?

What is the problem with the hole?

Who solves the problem? How?

Do you think Bob is smart?
Why or why not?

Is Bob a good pet?
What do you like about him?
Make a list.

Meet the Author-Illustrator
David McPhail

David McPhail started drawing when he was only two years old. He would draw with a black crayon on paper bags that his grandmother cut up for him. David thought this story was fun to write and draw. "I love how the pictures help a story take shape and make sense," he says.

Requests for permission to make copies of any part of the work should be submitted online at www.harcourt.com/contact or mailed to the following address: Permissions Department, Houghton Mifflin Harcourt Publishing Company, 6277 Sea Harbor Drive, Orlando, Florida 32887-6777.

www.HarcourtBooks.com

First Green Light Readers edition 2008

Green Light Readers and its logo are trademarks of Harcourt, Inc., registered in the United States of America and/or other jurisdictions.

Library of Congress Cataloging-in-Publication Data
McPhail, David, 1940–
Dot and Bob/David McPhail.
p. cm.
"Green Light Readers."
Summary: When Dot's mother begins to plant a tree Bob the dog decides to help.
[1. Dogs—Fiction. 2. Pets—Fiction.] I. Title.
PZ7.M2427Do 2008
[E]—dc22 2007042338
ISBN 978-0-15-206547-8
ISBN 978-0-15-206541-6 (pb)

A C E G H F D B
A C E G H F D B (pb)

Ages 4–6
Grade: I
Guided Reading Level: C
Reading Recovery Level: 3

Green Light Readers
For the reader who's ready to GO!

Five Tips to Help Your Child Become a Great Reader

1. Get involved. Reading aloud to and with your child is just as important as encouraging your child to read independently.

2. Be curious. Ask questions about what your child is reading.

3. Make reading fun. Allow your child to pick books on subjects that interest her or him.

4. Words are everywhere—not just in books. Practice reading signs, packages, and cereal boxes with your child.

5. Set a good example. Make sure your child sees YOU reading.

Why Green Light Readers Is the Best Series for Your New Reader

• Created exclusively for beginning readers by some of the biggest and brightest names in children's books

• Reinforces the reading skills your child is learning in school

• Encourages children to read—and finish—books by themselves

• Offers extra enrichment through fun, age-appropriate activities unique to each story

• Incorporates characteristics of the Reading Recovery program used by educators

• Developed with Harcourt School Publishers and credentialed educational consultants

Daniel's Pet
Alma Flor Ada/G. Brian Karas

Sometimes
Keith Baker

A New Home
Tim Bowers

A Big Surprise
Kristi T. Butler/Pamela Paparone

Rip's Secret Spot
Kristi T. Butler/Joe Cepeda

Get Up, Rick!
F. Isabel Campoy/Bernard Adnet

Sid's Surprise
Candace Carter/Joung Un Kim

Cloudy Day Sunny Day
Donald Crews

Jan Has a Doll
Janice Earl/Tricia Tusa

Rabbit and Turtle Go to School
Lucy Floyd/Christopher Denise

The Tapping Tale
Judy Giglio/Joe Cepeda

The Big, Big Wall
Reginald Howard/Ariane Dewey/Jose Aruego

Sam and the Bag
Alison Jeffries/Dan Andreasen

The Hat
Holly Keller

The Van
Holly Keller

What I See
Holly Keller

Down on the Farm
Rita Lascaro

Big Brown Bear
David McPhail

Big Pig and Little Pig
David McPhail

Dot and Bob
David McPhail

Jack and Rick
David McPhail

Rick Is Sick
David McPhail

Best Friends
Anna Michaels/G. Brian Karas

Come Here, Tiger!
Alex Moran/Lisa Campbell Ernst

Lost!
Alex Moran/Daniel Moreton

Popcorn
Alex Moran/Betsy Everitt

Sam and Jack: Three Stories
Alex Moran/Tim Bowers

Six Silly Foxes
Alex Moran/Keith Baker

What Day Is It?
Alex Moran/Daniel Moreton

Todd's Box
Paula Sullivan/Nadine Bernard Westcott

The Picnic
David K. Williams/Laura Ovresat

Tick Tock
David K. Williams/Laura Ovresat

Look for more Green Light Readers wherever books are sold!